ardman
Presents

Wallace & Gromit ™

Welcome to
West Wallaby Street

Nice to see you! Come in. Come in. Mind the step when you wipe your feet.

Written by Ro... ...rated by Bill Kerwin

WALLACE'S
WASH 'N' GO
WINDOW CLEANING
SERVICE

CRIME AND
PUNISHMENT

FIDO
DOGSTOYEVSKY

Right ho. Action stations, Gromit lad! Let's show our visitor how it works, shall we?
Bit of a dog-in-sheep's-clothing is our Gromit, but he's got quite a lot of bounce in him, I will say that...

Gromit getting canned!

SMASHING TIME IN SCUNTHORPE

Mayhem struck Scunthorpe-on-Tees' annual classical seaside music festival yesterday when a mechanical digger competing in a sandcastle-building competition nearby went berserk and began smashing up everything in sight. "The Diggatron has a very sensitive mechanism, and it would appear that Beethoven was not to its taste," explained the inventor.

RUSTLING RASCAL GETS LIFE!

Spectators crowding the public gallery during day six of the now infamous Sheep Dog Trial witnessed a dramatic turn of events when the judge overturned the defence's case and sentenced the accused, Gromit, to life imprisonment. Summing up, the judge said that Gromit, unemployed of 62 West Wallaby Street, was a menace to society in general and sheep in particular and should therefore serve the maximum sentence for his crimes.

Gromit being framed

Prepare for blast-off!

Cheese-tasting on the Moon

OCAL DUO NAB DASTARDLY
DIAMOND THIEF!

HOUND HAS THE
BOTTLE TO FOIL RAID

DOG LICENCE

NO: 44320

BUS TICKET
WENSLEYDALE

Where's the snap of our lunar voyage to show our guest, Gromit?
I could have sworn we had a shot of the rocket taking off in here somewhere.

Still, no time to look for it now. It's almost 16:21 hours. Shopper 13 should be on its return voyage. Let's get ourselves to the viewing platforms to witness its re-entry...